I LOVE OUR EARTH

I LOVE OUR PEOPLE

Carol Greene

Enslow Elementary, an imprint of Enslow Publishers, Inc.
Enslow Elementary® is a registered trademark of Enslow Publishers, Inc.

Library of Congress Cataloging-in-Publication Data

Greene, Carol.
  I love our people / by Carol Greene.
    p. cm. — (I love our earth)
  Includes index.
  Summary: "Find out why people are important, and how we can protect each other"—Provided by publisher.
  ISBN 978-0-7660-4041-0
  1. Human ecology—Juvenile literature. 2. Human beings—Effect of environment on—Juvenile literature. I. Title.
  GF48.G728 2012
  304.2—dc23
                        2011023714

Future editions:
Paperback ISBN 978-1-4644-0136-7
ePUB ISBN 978-1-4645-1043-4
PDF ISBN 978-1-4646-1043-1

Printed in the United States of America

032012 Lake Book Manufacturing, Inc., Melrose Park, IL

10 9 8 7 6 5 4 3 2 1

To Our Readers: We have done our best to make sure all Internet Addresses in this book were active and appropriate when we went to press. However, the author and the publisher have no control over and assume no liability for the material available on those Internet sites or on other Web sites they may link to. Any comments or suggestions can be sent by e-mail to comments@enslow.com or to the address on the back cover.

♻ Enslow Publishers, Inc., is committed to printing our books on recycled paper. The paper in every book contains 10% to 30% post-consumer waste (PCW). The cover board on the outside of each book contains 100% PCW. Our goal is to do our part to help young people and the environment too!

Photo Credits: Photos.com: Liquidlibrary, p. 21, Morgan Lane Studios, p. 1, Rich Legg, p. 11, Stockbyte, pp. 18–19, Thinkstock Images, p. 4; Shutterstock.com, pp. 3, 7, 8, 12–13, 15, 16, 24.

Cover Photo: Photos.com/Morgan Lane Studios

Enslow Elementary
an imprint of
Enslow Publishers, Inc.
40 Industrial Road
Box 398
Berkeley Heights, NJ 07922
USA
http://www.enslow.com

Contents

People live in different places all over the world. This family lives on a farm.

What Are They?

They need the earth to stay alive. The earth gives them many good things.

Sometimes they take care of the earth. Sometimes they don't.

What are they? People.

More than seven billion people live on the earth. They live in cities and towns, on farms, in the mountains, in deserts and on islands, and many other places.

Some people are rich. Many have enough money. But many are so poor that they are always hungry. Some even starve to death.

Why Are People Important?

People are important because of all they can do. They can think and feel. They can laugh and cry. They can love one another, and they can love the earth.

People are important because they can help take care of the earth. They can plant trees and gardens and crops. They can save wild animals and care for tame animals. They can keep the earth clean.

People take care of many kinds of animals. This girl is feeding a baby tiger in a zoo in Bangkok.

People can love the earth by
spending time outdoors.

People can enjoy the earth. They can show and tell how beautiful it is. They can write poems, stories, and music about the earth. They can dance dances and paint pictures.

People are important because of all they can do. But they are also important just because they are.

Each person is alive. Each is different. Each is beautiful, and each is important.

What Can Happen to People?

If people do not take care of the earth and of each other, bad things can happen.

In Haiti, people cut down too many trees. The soil wore away, and crops could not grow. Now many people in Haiti do not have enough to eat.

In the United States, people put poison wastes in the ground near a town. The wastes got into the soil and people in the town had to leave their homes.

In hard times, people may lose their homes. This man is living on the street.

In India, some people made a mistake at a factory. Poison gas got into the air and killed many people.

Along the Gulf Coast, an oil drilling rig exploded and spilled millions of gallons of oil into the water. It killed many animals. Beaches looked ugly and people felt sad and angry.

People need the earth for food and homes. They need clean air and clean water. They need beautiful things to see and love.

But if they do not take care of the earth, people will lose these things.

The Gulf Coast oil spill spread to hundreds of miles of beaches. This is a beach in Gulf Shores, Alabama.

What Can We Do?

Some people have already harmed the earth and one another. Often they do this because they are greedy. They want lots of things. They don't care about others.

But people can change. They can think about the earth and how it works. They can think about others and what they need.

People can also think about all the people who haven't been born yet. They should have a clean, beautiful earth, too.

The earth can give people many things. This boy is holding apples from a tree.

People must take care of the earth. Riding bikes instead of driving saves fuel and makes the air cleaner.

People must stop putting pollutants into the air, soil, and water. Pollutants are harmful things left over after burning or making something. People can make things in cleaner, safer ways.

People can stop cutting down too many trees. They can leave room for the plants and animals. People can stop using so much oil and coal. They can find other fuels.

If people do these things, others may lose their jobs. Then we can help them find new jobs that do not harm the earth.

We must also help poor people now. We can give them food and help them find ways to get their own food. We must help poor people find ways to earn money so everyone can live a heathy, happy life.

Many groups of people are working together to make a better earth. Some work for animals; some for air, water, or forests; and some for people. But they all want the same thing—a better earth.

It will take a lot of work to make the earth better. All the people in the world will have to work together. It will take time and money. But it will be worth it.

What Can You Do?

You can help other people, too. You can work for a better earth. Here are some things that you can do.

★ 1. Learn more about the earth and how different things work together. Get books from the library. Watch nature shows on TV or on the Web. Talk to your family and friends about what you have learned.

★ 2. Hold a fund-raiser. Donate the money to a local charity that helps people.

★ 3. Write a poem or story, draw a picture, sing a song, or dance a dance that shows how much you love the earth. Share what you do with other people.

★ 4. Learn about people in other countries. How are they different from you? How are they the same?

★ 5. Be very, very kind to the people around you.

Show how much
you care for the
earth and people.
Plant a tree with
someone you love!

Words to Know

fuel (FYOOL)—Something people burn to get heat or power.

greedy—Wanting to have too much.

Gulf Coast—The southeast part of the United States that is along the Gulf of Mexico.

Haiti (HATE ee)—A small island country near Cuba.

India—A large country in southern Asia.

oil—A greasy liquid that can be burned as fuel.

poison (POYZ un)—A thing that is harmful to people, animals, and plants.

soil—A mix of ground-up rock, dead plants and animals, air, and water.

starve—To die from not having food.

waste—A thing left over after burning or making something.

Learn More

Books

O'Ryan, Ellie. *Easy to Be Green: Simple Activities You Can Do to Save the Earth.* New York: Simon & Schuster, 2009.

Parr, Todd. *The Earth Book.* Boston: Little, Brown Books for Young Readers, 2010.

Slade, Suzanne. *What Can We Do About Pollution?* New York: PowerKids Press, 2009.

Threadgould, Tiffany. *ReMake It! Recycling Projects From the Stuff You Usually Scrap.* New York: Sterling, 2011.

Web Sites

EPA: Recycle City.
<http://www.epa.gov/recyclecity/>

Save the Earth for Kids.
<http://www.SaveTheEarthForKids.com>

Index